The King of Capri

by Jeanette Winterson

illustrated by Jane Ray

BLOOMSBURY
CHILDREN'S
BOOKS

The King of Capri had been out to a party.
It was just the kind of party that Kings like best. All his friends were there,
and somebody had cooked his favorite food. There was royal jelly,
crown of lamb, queen of puddings, buns with pearly icing, and
chocolate soldiers. The King ate as much as he could but
not as much as he would have liked. He had a bun
in onc hand, jelly in the other hand, but try
as he might, he couldn't get all the
jelly and all the bun into
his mouth at

once.

"Why have I got two hands but only one mouth?" wondered the King.
His advisor stood before him and said, "Sire, think of all the poor people
in your kingdom. They can hardly feed one mouth each.
However could they feed two?"
But the King never did think about the poor people.
He thought only about himself.

It was midnight when the King got back to his palace. All his servants were asleep. The King looked at himself in the mirror and saw that he was covered in ice cream and treacle and egg sandwich and orange juice and bits of banana.

"If I had two mouths," he said to himself, "I shouldn't be in this mess. How can anybody be expected to get all their food into just one mouth?"

Well, what could he do? He took off all his dirty clothes, except for his socks and his crown, then he padded out onto the balcony and pegged his clothes on the line. He had often seen clothes hanging on the line. He didn't know that you have to wash them first.

Then the King got into his big bed and fell asleep.

Capri is an island. The King's palace sat high up on a cliff that looked out to sea.
Very often the King would lean on his balcony and admire the view over the Bay
of Naples. Across the bay was the city of Naples, where a lot of poor people lived.
The poorest of them all was a washerwoman called Mrs. Jewel.

If you went to Mrs. Jewel's house to look
for her, you wouldn't be able to see her.
For a start, Mrs. Jewel was very small, and
her tiny house was always full of steam.
This was because she did her washing in
a great big boiler, and all day long the
boiler boiled and boiled, while Mrs. Jewel
threw in the dirty clothes and hauled out the clean
ones, and never got her head out of the steam.

There were people who had known her for years
and had no idea of what she looked like. All they
ever saw was a little column of steam moving
about through the big columns of steam.

Mrs. Jewel had a cat. The cat was called Wash.

It was midnight. Mrs. Jewel and Wash had just finished their supper. Mrs. Jewel had eaten a chicken wing, nineteen baked beans, a tomato, and half a slice of bread. Then they were going to share a cup of milk.

"Two mouths to feed, Wash," said Mrs. Jewel. "But only one supper."

Wash rubbed his head against her hand. He was the thinnest cat in the world. He was so thin that if he swallowed a mouse it made a big bulge in his tummy, like carrying a tennis ball in your pocket.

No matter how hard Mrs. Jewel worked, she never had enough money, because although everyone wanted clean clothes, no one wanted to pay much for them. "Never mind," she thought. "I will do my best, and someday all this will change."

That night a great tempest blew in across the sea.

On Capri, where the King was snoring loudly in his crown and his socks, the first thing that the Wind did was to blow the peaked caps off the palace guards.

And the second thing that the Wind did was to blow the birds out of the trees.

And the third thing that the Wind did was to blow all the deck chairs off the beach.

And the fourth thing that the Wind did was to blow the hands off the church clock.

And the fifth thing that the Wind did was to blow the mustaches off the night watchmen.

And the sixth thing that the Wind did was to blow the wigs off the ladies-in-waiting.

And the seventh thing that the Wind did was to blow the pajamas off all the King's men.

And the eighth thing that the Wind did was to blow all the milk out of the cows.

And the ninth thing that the Wind did was to blow all the King's clothes off his balcony.

If you had looked over the Bay of Naples that night, you would have seen the King's velvet breeches

and the King's silk shirt and the King's golden waistcoat

and the King's embroidered cloak all flying across the sea.

And where do you think they landed?

They landed on Mrs. Jewel's washing line but she doesn't know that yet.

Never in all
the history of Capri
had there been such a wind.
Everyone was woken up, except for
the King, who was so fat and so weighed
down with buns and jelly that even a tempest
couldn't so much as blow his hair across the pillow.
Perhaps that was because his hair was stuck to the pillow with a
jam sandwich he kept underneath it at night, in case he got hungry.
By morning the news was out. Every single thing in Capri, every pot,
pan, coat hanger, chicken, and lottery ticket had been blown away.
And where do you think they had all landed?
It was Wash who found out first.

Wash had woken up on a pile of towels where he wasn't supposed to be sleeping. He yawned and stretched himself, and as it was daylight, he thought he'd go for a walk outside. Mrs. Jewel had a big backyard where she dried all her laundry, and when Wash had finished walking and sniffing and rolling and looking and all the things that cats like to do, he lay down high up on the wall, his body as orange as the sun and his eyes like two gold coins.

The Wind was outside.

"Good morning, Wash," said the Wind.

"*Buon giorno,*" said Wash, by which Italian cats mean Good morning.

"I had a bit of a night last night," said the Wind. "I'm sorry about all the stuff in your backyard."

"*Non c'è di che,*" said Wash, who wasn't taking any notice and who just said, "Don't mention it."

Then Wash looked. Then he looked again.
Then he looked again and again.

It looked as if the whole world had piled
itself up in Mrs. Jewel's backyard. There was a
bed with somebody still asleep in it.

On top of the bed was a cow.

On top of the cow was a vacuum cleaner.

On top of the vacuum cleaner was a bicycle.

On top of the bicycle was a box of apples.

On top of the apples was a duck.

On top of the duck was a pair of knickers.

On top of the pair of knickers was a big pan
of chicken soup.

"I'll eat that," said Wash.

He climbed up and while he was slurping from the pan, he realized that everything he had ever seen in his life was piled up in the backyard.

"I didn't know where else to put it," said the Wind. "You do these things in a moment of madness and then you're left with the mess."

But Wash didn't answer because he was too busy eating.

"I'll clear it up later," said the Wind. "Goodbye, Wash."

"*Ciao,*" said Wash, by which Italian cats mean Goodbye.

The Wind flew off and everything was still.
When Mrs. Jewel came out with her first
load of laundry, she saw Wash, round as a
ball, and fast asleep on a pair of knickers.
And she saw that the whole world was in
her backyard.

"Well I'll be blowed," she said.

Now Wash and Mrs. Jewel were rich. They
had everything they needed, but best of all,
Mrs. Jewel had a new suit of clothes.

"These are fit for a King," she said, when she
saw the velvet breeches, the silk shirt, the gold
waistcoat and the embroidered cloak. She soon
had the stains out, and when she put on the
clothes, she looked like – well, what do you
think she looked like? She looked like a Queen!

News soon spread that there was a Queen come to Naples who had all the treasure in the world in her backyard. Every morning she sat on an upturned laundry basket and graciously received her visitors. To the rich, she gave advice, and to the poor she gave money.

She had plenty of money because Wash had found the King's treasure chest underneath a box of fish.

What of the King of Capri?

Well, he and everybody who lived on the island were now as poor as the people of Naples had been before the wind blew everything across the sea. The King had nothing to wear but his socks and his crown and an old dressing gown that belonged to the gardener. He had nothing to eat either, except what he could grow in the garden or catch from the sea. All his servants and all his friends gradually left him one by one to work for the Queen of Naples. She was building a palace in her backyard.

Soon the King was the only person left on the island. He was lonely and sad and thin.

"How glad I am that I have only one mouth to feed," he said to himself. "If I had two mouths I should be twice as hungry."

And he thought of all the food he had wasted and thrown away, and of the many times he had refused to give the beggars anything to eat.

Then one day when his plate was empty, he swallowed his pride and rowed across the bay to see the Queen of Naples.

How splendid everything looked on the glittering coastline.

There were market stalls selling fresh bread and people running about building things and making things.

Everyone seemed happy and full.

When he asked the way to the Queen's house, they told him how good and kind and generous she was, and the King remembered that no one had ever said that about him. He came to the marvelous palace and there was an enormous orange cat sitting on the front step.

"Is the Queen at home?" asked the King.

"*Si, si, si,*" said Wash, by which Italian cats mean Yes.

The King could hear somebody singing, so he went round the back and there was Mrs. Jewel, now Queen of Naples, standing over a steaming tub and washing her nightdress.

"Have you no servants?" asked the King.

"Hundreds," said the Queen. "But where's the fun in that?"

"I used to have servants once," said the King. Then he looked closely at Mrs. Jewel. "Come to think of it, I used to have a suit of clothes just like the ones you are wearing."

"What, just like these?" said the Queen.

"Well, mine had a few stains on them, it's true."

And then the King told the story of how every single thing on his island had been blown away by a tempest.

"Wash!" shouted the Queen. "Come here! Do you know anything about a tempest?"

Wash slunk round the corner and had to tell the whole story about how the Wind had dropped everything from Capri into Mrs. Jewel's backyard, including the King's clothes.

"Well, you'd better take it all back then, hadn't you?" said Mrs. Jewel to the King.

"But what would you do then?" asked the King.

"Oh, go back to the laundry business, I suppose," said Mrs. Jewel. "Only I wouldn't want Wash to be hungry again."

The King was silent for a while, and while he was silent he was looking at the sunshine and the flowers and wondering why he never used to look at them before. Then he looked at Mrs. Jewel and thought she was as lovely as sunshine and flowers and that if she were with him he would be happy and good for the rest of his life.

He said, "When I was King of Capri, I used to long for two mouths so that I could eat twice as much food. I should like two mouths now — my own, and yours to talk to me. My own, and yours to smile at me. My own, and yours to kiss good morning and to kiss good night."

And the King asked Mrs. Jewel to marry him, and what do you think she said?

The King and Mrs. Jewel were married in great style and everyone from Naples and Capri was invited, and everyone had enough to eat and a present to take home.

The best guest of all was Wash's old friend, the Wind, who carefully blew everybody's possessions back to the right place, so that the bed went back to the bedroom, and the cow went back to her field, and the vacuum cleaner went back in the cupboard, and the bicycle went riding down the road, and the apples, well, they had been eaten, and the duck went back to her pond, and the knickers went back in the drawer, and the pan of soup, well, that had been eaten, too.

And Wash, who had eaten it, on that very first morning when the Wind made a Queen of Mrs. Jewel, licked his lips and lay on the wall, his fur as orange as the sun, and his eyes like two gold coins.